'90s KINDA LOVE

LAY YOUR HEAD ON MY PILLOW

I0705948

TANZANIA GLOVER

Copyright © 2020 by Tanzania Glover

First Edition. 2020.

This is a work of fiction. Names, characters, businesses, places, events and incidents are either the products of the author's imagination or used in a fictitious manner. Any resemblance to actual persons, living or dead, or actual events is purely coincidental.

Cover Art by Scheba Derogene

www.tanzaniaglover.com

Booking With Love
332 S Michigan Ave

Suite #121- 2217
Chicago, IL 60604
www.bookingwithlove.com

I dedicate this to the four amazingly talented women who worked on this anthology with me.

Thanks for being there and encouraging me through the last few months because I would have gone mad if it weren't for the distraction that this project provided me with or all of the laughs and ideas shared in our group chat.

In one way or another life tried its best to knock us all down, but we never gave up and I'm so proud of us for not only getting it done but getting it done well and making it look easy. This experience was truly a pleasure and I can't wait to read all of those drafted story ideas that this project spawned.

We made it!

Listen to the playlist!

'90S KINDA LOVE *LAY YOUR HEAD ON MY PILLOW*

Toni...

Nothing exciting ever happened to me. Not even on my birthday. That's why when I woke up that morning then put my pants on one leg at a time, I expected it to be a day just like any other day pushing certain kids to take a chance on their dream college while unfortunately reminding others to be more realistic about their options. Following in my late mother's footsteps, I had been Lakewood High's resident guidance counselor for the better part of a decade, but the time had flown by so quickly that I often wondered where it had gone and what exactly I'd done with it.

This job was supposed to be temporary, you know just something to put on the old resumé before I went back to school to settle on what I really wanted to do with my life, but before I had known it I was in my mid-thirties and still stuck in Long Beach and in the same unsatisfying routine that had begun at twenty-five. Oh yeah and I still hadn't quite figured out what I wanted to do yet.

But despite my obvious complaining, I did generally enjoy what I did because I got to do my part to shape the futures of brilliant young minds and I was allowed to work alongside my best friend since training bras and spray painted t-shirts. To everyone else she was Principal Jillian Brooks, but to me she was currently the heifer who had set me up on one too many bad dates.

Now *I* didn't have a problem with my singleness at all, but after hitting thirty-five Jill was officially on a schedule that would include a husband and a baby any year now and since we had done everything else together she wanted those things to be no exception for us. So far the only thing getting in her way was that I was something like a picky eater only if you replaced *eater* with *dater*.

For the life of me I couldn't tell anybody what my type was because in the past I usually just knew it when I saw it. And after finally admitting that she couldn't pick a guy for me any better than I could, Jill convinced me to try online dating. But after striking out with every man that I'd matched with, I deleted the apps and tried to get back used to being home again on Friday nights.

Jill didn't let me rest for long though because her latest bright idea was trying to set me up with the artist who had been commissioned to replace the school's mural last week. It had been covered for some time now after being vandalized by a local gang, but unbeknownst to me Jill had finally found the perfect man for the job and possibly the perfect man for me.

Despite him being something like a celebrity around these Southern California parts, Arlan Parks had surprisingly given an enthusiastic yes to the offer and even refused the payment from the district. We had assumed that it was because he was a former Lakewood student and that he wanted to do something nice for his old stomping grounds, but the real reason would hit a lot closer to home than anybody could've known.

Now I wouldn't deny that he was a very attractive man and the idea of taking a sip of that tall, dark drink of water was certainly enticing, but all of that was cancelled out by the fact that he practically still had milk on his tongue. He had only graduated the year before I was hired here which had to put him at around twenty-seven or twenty-eight, either of which would have me feeling like I was robbing the cradle so I nixed the idea before Jill could even finish plotting on a way to get it done.

Or at least that was what I'd thought because I should have already known that she had something to do with him continuously finding excuses to come by my office all week. At first it was because he kept "forgetting" where the art room that stored his supplies was and for the past few days it'd been to use my private bathroom.

Finally I decided to politely let him know that he was actually passing a faculty men's room on his way to me so that he didn't have to keep walking so far out of his way.

"You've never been in a men's room before, have you Ms.

Riley?" he asked me with remnants of boyish charm in his crooked smile as he finished drying his hands.

"No. Can't say that I have, Mr. Parks."

"Well just trust me then. There's a reason why I'd prefer to continue using yours if you don't mind. At least it's one of the reasons," he added on before tossing the napkin in the trash.

"And what are the other reasons?" I asked curiously as I comfortably leaned back in my chair, but I didn't get an answer because at that very moment a couple of my favorite students decided to come bursting through the door.

"Will! Kayla! What did I tell you guys about not knocking first?" I asked before seeing that they were just trying to surprise me with balloons and the giant birthday card that only the seniors were allowed to sign. It had been a tradition since my first year here and I still had all of the others in the back of my closet at home.

"Oooh Ms. Riley got a man in here y'all and he's cute," Kayla said to the few students behind her as she sat everything down then quickly backed out of my office and closed the door.

"Sorry about that," I said to

Arlan even though she wasn't exactly lying since he did put the *fine* in fine artist.

"That's okay. Kids will be kids," he remarked and I had to fight the urge to say that of course he would understand because he was almost still one himself. "Oh and Happy Birthday."

"Thank you. Is there something else that I can help you with, Mr. Parks?" I asked him in an even tone when I realized that he hadn't made a move for the door how he usually did when he was finished.

Instead he had come closer and took a seat at the chair

opposite my desk. And even though he had already been out in the sweltering sun for hours today, I could still smell the irresistible scent of his cologne mixed with his sweat.

"Yeah. I've been meaning to ask you about that," he said pointing to the framed quote that hung next to my degrees and a few work appropriate pictures of family and friends. "What does that mean to you?"

I had noticed him looking passed me a couple times when he was briefly in here before, but I smiled when I knew that I finally had the answer to what he had been fixated on.

I didn't have to glance over my shoulder to see it because the simple phrase had been etched into my brain from reading it daily, but I did it anyway.

The words, *Collect Beautiful Moments*, were ones that I was supposed to be living by since losing my mother because they had stopped me in my tracks when I saw them on my weekly Target run five years ago. But alas I had collected nothing but Netflix shows, a few pounds that I didn't need and an assortment of wine glasses since then.

"I think it's pretty self-explanatory, but to me it means to have all the experiences and maybe stop and take a few pictures along the way to have something to remember."

"And are you doing any of that?" he asked probably not intentionally trying to excite my internal senses, but the way the sleeveless paint and sweat covered shirt clung to his body and outlined his well-maintained physique was really a sight to see. I could tell that he knew the effect his looks had on women, but there was no air of arrogance coming from him and I liked that.

I cleared my throat once I realized that I had been quiet and staring at him for a second too long.

"Not yet, to be honest. But I will. At least I've been planning to one day soon."

"With all due respect, Ms. Riley," he began then smiled when he reached out and touched my gilded name plate, "Or can I just call you Toni? Ms. Riley makes it sound like I'm still a student here."

"You're not exactly too far removed," I teased him about his age and his smile widened, "But Toni is fine."

"Yeah she is," he said forwardly then let me know that I could also stop being so formal and to use his first name as well. I was at a loss for words though and I couldn't make my mouth form any so I just nodded in agreement before he went on.

"So like I was saying, and again with all due respect, but what you're saying is a load of crap," he said then watched me closely to see my natural reaction. "You can't just *plan* to collect beautiful moments. Beautiful moments just happen. They're the kind of thing that just falls into your lap when you least expect it, you know?" he asked waiting for my co-sign, but I wholeheartedly disagreed because I had thirty-five years of nothing even attempting to fall in the direction of my lap let alone in it.

"No. I've been waiting for something to happen my whole life and it never has so now I'm of the opinion that I'll just have to create the moments that I want to collect."

He smiled at me standing my ground then just when he went to dig his heels in to further the debate, another disruptive barge in took place. This time it was Jill and she too smiled at the sight before her, Arlan and I alone and clearly having an engaging conversation by how we were both leaning towards one another over my desk.

"Oh excuse me for

interrupting, Ms. Riley," she said and I grinned to myself because she only called me that when we were in the presence of students.

"No, it's fine, Ms. Brooks. Mr. Parks," I began before catching his eye. "I mean Arlan was just on his way out."

"Was I really, Toni?" he asked with that crooked grin again and I saw the little twinkle in Jill's eyes at the way he said my name. She was about to make her move.

"Well if you haven't eaten yet I was just about to take *Toni* out for a nice birthday lunch. Care to join us?" she asked extending an invitation to him, but he still looked in my direction for permission which he quickly got with another nod because words were still escaping me.

"Thanks I'd like that. But as much as I hate to say no to the beautiful birthday girl, I'm not exactly dressed for the occasion," he remarked looking down at his sweat stains only I was now focused on how casually he'd just called me beautiful. Like it was just an understood and accepted fact.

Today was my birthday. And I was beautiful.

"Well how about tonight then?" Jill asked us both. "That should give you plenty of time to clean up nicely and take her out for a birthday dinner."

"Jill!" I nearly shrieked because she was somehow being even more forward than he was on my behalf. "You'll have to excuse her. She wasn't dropped on her head as a baby, but she will be the second we leave," I casually threatened her.

"No, that's alright," he said sounding amused at us. "I'm glad she said it because I've been chickening out every time I come in here. You know how much water I've been drinking just to have an excuse to make small talk with you these last few days?" he asked me like we were the only two in the room and soon enough we were because Jill pretended to forget her wallet in her office.

I was sure that he knew like I knew that it was just an excuse to give us a moment to set up an official time and place to meet up later, but to my surprise he asked if I wanted to come by his place for dinner and drinks. Even though I was positive that he had some big, fancy famous artist's house, it still didn't change the fact that I didn't go to strange men's homes for dates. Even if you set clear boundaries from the gate there would still always be an assumption about what would be on the menu for dessert.

Like he was reading my

mind, he added, "I promise it wouldn't be anything like that. Just dinner and maybe a quick painting lesson so we can replace that," he said nodding over to the wall with the quote. "You know since you're not exactly using it correctly," he quipped before jotting down his number and address on a post-it from my desk.

"Thanks for the alley-oop, Ms. Brooks. Couldn't have done it without you," he said to a newly reappeared Jill on his way out.

"Anytime," she replied as she looked after him for a second too long then closed my door and turned to me. "Toni Riley, you better do the right thing with that youngin' because those are the kind of sloppy seconds that I would ruin my oldest friendship for," she joked as she playfully fanned herself.

"Oh don't you worry. I'm already planning on it," I told her confidently as I grabbed my purse then followed after her.

Before we were out of the door I looked back to see the time on the clock, but instead the quote caught my eye again. I decided to take it as a sign from the universe that my spur of the moment plans to collect something beautiful from Arlan later on tonight were a go.

♫ ♫ ♫

Picking out clothes for work that morning had been as easy as it always was because even though it was my birthday it was still just another day. A nice, light blouse and slacks was appropriate for any occasion and had me looking cute but professional on the daily.

But now that I would be spending the evening with the beautiful specimen of a man that was Arlan Parks I knew that I couldn't just show up in what he'd been seeing me in all week. I needed to wow him, but I figured that pulling out one of my rarely worn *freakum* dresses would be a little too bold.

I settled on a fitted, black tank dress that I made look more special than it was with a few key accessories and a long floral shawl. It was enough to make him look twice, but also something that I wouldn't mind tossing because we would be painting at some point.

I didn't know what I expected when I put his address into my GPS, but when I arrived at my destination I was sure that I was in the wrong place. I just knew that he would be living in some gritty but expensive industrial brick loft, but after double checking the address on the post-it I knew I was where I was supposed to be.

Belmont Shore wasn't a typical suburb and felt more like an extension of Long Beach because of all the bars and young professionals who lived there, but it still didn't seem like the kind of place a man like him would call home because it was too normal. But I tucked all of those thoughts away along with the bag of special art supplies I'd picked up on my way home from work before darkening his doorstep five minutes passed seven.

Even though I hadn't gone

with a revealing dress, I could still tell that he was pleased with my appearance because he eagerly opened the door before I could finish knocking then gave me an appreciative once over.

"Wow Toni. You look…" he began then stepped aside to let me in and marvel over my hair. The long, thick rope twists that I'd worn in a low bun all week were unraveled to create a gravity defying kinky-curly fro that looked like it was trying to touch the night sky. "I can't even find the words. Happy Birthday!" he said again instead.

"Thanks," I said as I took in all the wonderful smells of dinner permeating the air. I was glad that I had brought some reinforcements for breath control because I was picking up a garlicy steak aroma that I would soon be devouring since I had been too nervous about tonight to even eat the lunch Jill had treated me to earlier.

"Can I take your…um what is that, a kimono?" he asked being silly as I sat the black shopping bag down by my feet then slipped out of the shawl.

"No, it's a wrap."

"What's in the bag? You didn't have to bring me anything. Just your company was enough."

"It's nothing. A little paint

and other stuff for us to use for the lesson tonight."

"Paint? Toni, I don't know if you somehow forgot, but I'm kind of a professional painter. I have acrylic, oil, watercolor, gouache, and even some encaustic. You just brought sand to the beach."

"No, the saleswoman assured me that this paint would be a little different than anything you might have here."

"That's what they all say. Let me see it," he said as he went for the bag, but I quickly stepped in front of it bringing us nose-to-nose or rather his nose to the top of my head because he stood much taller than my five-foot-five *with* wedges on frame. I hadn't taken the time to appreciate his height before because I was always seated when he came into my office, but I was even more attracted to him seeing how he towered over me now.

"Later. Be patient and I promise it'll be worth the wait," I assured him even though being so close to him was making me feel like saying to hell with dinner and showing him my plans a little earlier than I'd wanted to at first.

I could tell that the feeling was mutual by his refusal to take a step back out of my personal space, but just like every other time we had been alone today there was another interruption. I was almost startled by a man's voice coming from what I guessed was the kitchen.

"Table's set, AP! Just take the mousse out of the freezer a few minutes before serving it and you'll be good," said an equally tall but chubbier man with a little urgency in his voice as he joined us in the entryway of the house. The navy blue chef's coat that he wore made me put his previous words into context. "Hey who's this?" he asked looking me over as well.

"Hi, I'm Toni Riley," I told him then stuck out my hand for a shake after he'd secured a big bag of what I could only describe as chef stuff on his back.

"Toni Riley?" he asked like it sounded familiar instead of telling me his name. "Hey you wouldn't be related to Tess Riley, would you? Doesn't she kind of look like Ms. Riley, that old guidance counselor from Lakewood?" he asked Arlan, but I answered again before he could.

"She's actually my mom. Well *was* my mom. I mean she's still my mom, but she's no longer living. She passed away some years ago," I let out quietly after realizing how much I was saying to such a simple observation.

Sensing my comfort levels

suddenly plunging, Arlan began rushing the man out of the door again.

"Hey Dave, don't you have somewhere to be soon, man?"

"Oh right. Nice meeting you Toni and uh…sorry about your mom. She was a cool lady. Enjoy the food," he barely got out before Arlan was closing the door on him.

"I'm not usually that rude, but he'll talk forever if you let him and his dad really needed him for something tonight."

"It's fine. Is he your roommate?" I asked curiously because I could tell from the layout of the house that there were at least two bedrooms on the first floor.

"No. I live here alone. He's just a buddy from high school that I get to cook for me on holidays and special occasions," he said as he finally led the way to the dining room and my eyes widened at the sight before me.

It was a rustic but still nicely presented spread of grilled shrimp and steak as well as a few hearty sides. But even aside from the food porn, the entire set up was so nice that I had to step outside of myself and temporarily be one of those *take a picture before I eat* kind of people. I promised him that I wouldn't share it with anybody except for maybe Jill, but he said he didn't mind as he pulled out a chair for me to sit in.

"I just figured that we would get a pizza or something before we started painting. You really didn't have to go through all of this trouble for me, Arlan."

"Dave owes me tons of favors so it was no trouble. And besides, we'll definitely get takeout at some point because I don't even know how to turn on my stove let alone cook on it," he chuckled out then continued sincerely with, "But tonight is your birthday and I thought you deserved a beautiful moment to collect."

"But I thought you said that beautiful moments couldn't be planned. That was your stance earlier, right?" I asked sarcastically then watched as his contagious smile spread across the table to infect me.

"For the most part I still think it's true, but then I thought about all the days I'd seen you since I started the mural," he began but paused as he uncorked the bottle of wine that had been chilling on the table, "and how if I hadn't *planned* to finally talk to you today then we wouldn't be sitting here together right now, would we?"

"Well if we let Jill tell it then

she did all the heavy lifting and you just swooped in for the credit," I joked because she hadn't actually said that.

"I guess I don't mind her getting the credit then as long as I can have the moment with you," he said sweetly.

"To Jill then," I suggested holding up my glass.

"To you," he said instead as he clinked his with mine. "On your what birthday?" he asked suddenly trying to gauge my age by looking at me.

"Thirty-fifth," I said proudly and he seemed surprised, but I was never one of those people who was scared to get older.

I welcomed the greys and the little bit of wisdom I had picked up over the years. I just didn't like that time was slipping through my fingers so quickly without me having anything to show for it. That, much more than aging could ever be, was my biggest fear.

"How old are you?" I asked him pointlessly because I had spent most of my time after work looking him up online and finding out as much as I could since I would be alone with him in his home.

I now knew that he was a student athlete suddenly turned artist in his final year of high school at Lakewood and that he had gone to UCLA's highly regarded art program. I'd even checked out his website and I really liked his work.

Of course I had a standard layman's knowledge of the arts, but an article from the *L.A. Times* about him told me that Arlan was separated from his peers because he skillfully used elements of both abstract expressionism as well as surrealism in his work. I guess that would explain why the price for just one of his pieces was a little more than my yearly salary.

"I'm twenty-seven, but I'll be twenty-eight in a few weeks if that bothers you," he offered up like it would make a big difference and I laughed.

"Why would it bother me? From the looks of things you seem mature for your age," I said pretty convincingly because his age had definitely factored into what I planned on doing with him tonight.

"Yeah, but I know a lot of women prefer to date older men in general."

"Date? Is this supposed to be a date? Because I believe I was told that this would be a painting lesson that just so happened to include a meal," I teased him just to see what he would say.

"Is that what you told your boyfriend?" he countered.

"I'm officially too old for a boyfriend today," I said purposely being coy.

"Well if by chance you do have a *man*, then boy did he mess up by letting me get a turn at bat tonight," he said confidently.

"You think so?" I asked playfully.

"Yeah. Don't let these paintbrushes and easels fool you, Toni. I'm still from Long Beach and I will Crip walk all over a dude trying to keep me away from you."

"That's cute. You know to be so young you sure do know all the right things to say to a woman. How are you still single?" I asked, but he clearly wasn't prepared for that question because he took a slow sip of wine while he thought about his answer. I decided to let him off the hook easily.

"I mean obviously I don't know you very well, but you did arrange all of this for a stranger who you're not even sure puts out so there must be a decent guy in there somewhere," I told him and he grinned then nodded in agreement as he sat his glass down.

"I guess I'm single because I'm a...I hate to use the term 'hopeless romantic' because it's not exactly like that. But I guess I have an idea in my head of how a relationship is supposed to feel and so far none of mine have ever even come close to feeling like that."

"Well what's your idea? How should it feel?" I asked and he was slow to answer again.

"I don't know how to say this without completely turning you off, but I think it should feel easy," he chuckled out nervously then went on. "I'm not naïve. I know all relationships will have their rough patches and growing pains, right? But why does maintaining one always have to feel like a job? I want to have the kind of relationship where even if there's chaos going on, at the end of the day it's still easy to choose her. Does that make sense?"

"Depends on what your definition of chaos is," I said because most men's idea of drama greatly differed from mine. That was probably the biggest reason why *I* was still single.

"Just life in general and whatever comes at us. I don't mean other women and that kind of thing," he assured me sounding sincere. "I just don't know why it has to be so hard."

"Well maybe that's how you'll know. It'll probably be easy when you finally meet the right one," I said then finally picked up my fork to take a bite of food because I had been dreamily getting lost in his glossy brown eyes while he spoke.

We continued the conversation and had a healthy debate about relationship dynamics, but I wasn't expecting him to bring up the elephant in the room at all let alone so soon in the evening.

"So why does Jill think somebody as beautiful as you are needs help getting a date, Toni?"

"It's not *getting* a date that's the problem. It's getting the *right* date that's proven difficult so far. And Jill...she's just invested because she wants us to experience the rest of our firsts together."

"Firsts?" he asked with lines forming on his forehead.

"Yeah you know, our *first* husbands, our *first* babies, that kind of thing," I said simply even though I had begun suspecting that Jill's motives ran a little deeper than that. She knew after losing my mother that I didn't have anybody else so she probably wanted to make sure that I wouldn't be alone while she was busy getting the rest of her firsts.

"And what do you want?" he asked what had to be his

hundredth question for the day. And even though I felt like they were borderline intrusive for somebody I'd just met, I decided to engage him because in spite of the messenger these were things that needed to be asked.

I sighed.

"I don't know. I guess I've spent the last ten years helping my kids sort out their futures just to have an excuse to avoid having to plan my own."

"Are you in therapy?" he asked suddenly.

"Why, does it seem like I need to be?"

"No, that just sounded like something a therapist would say.

It's good that you're so self-aware. Most people aren't these days," he said thoughtfully.

Throughout the rest of the meal I made sure not to eat too much not because I was trying to be cutesy for him. I just didn't want to get too full because the night was still in its infancy and I knew better than to potentially get *physical* on a full stomach. And I was almost certain that the *potential* part could be omitted because so far he was saying and doing all the right things and I was almost positive the night would end up exactly how I'd planned it to be.

After finishing the last drops

of the bottle of wine, he asked if I was ready to head to his studio. There were hardly any basements in California so I wasn't surprised to see that it was upstairs. He led the way but made sure to reach back for my hand like he was afraid I would get lost in this big place without him.

Right away I knew he'd had some remodeling done up here because there should have been at least a few rooms, but it was just one huge converted space now. But even more unusual than the layout was that it was neat. No splattered paint or messes anywhere which told me that he was either a serial killer or he took a lot of pride in keeping his space clear. I prayed for the latter.

I also couldn't help but notice that instead of artwork donning the walls he had puzzles hanging in between the large windows that brought in lots of natural light. But not just any puzzles. He had those gigantic 3,000 piece jigsaws and they told me he had patience like I couldn't begin to imagine so I had no choice but to ask about them.

"It's considered a little narcissistic to put your art up in your own house so I found a loophole. These were created out of some of the pieces that I would never sell to anybody," he said before giving me a painter's apron to keep me mess free, but he didn't bother with one.

I was about to thank him when he went to help me put it on. He was in front of me so he used his long arms to reach around and tie it from where he stood. I felt his warm breath on my face as he slowly doubled the knot as an excuse to have our bodies pressed together for a couple seconds longer.

"You're all set," he said then took a step back.

"You've done this before, haven't you? Brought a woman up here to make her feel like she's getting to see something from you that others haven't."

"Would you believe me if I said no?"

"No," I answered truthfully and he laughed.

"Well I haven't. My work is personal to me and I would never show this space to just anybody."

"So why me then? You don't even know me," I said being cheeky because the wine was finally hitting me, but he furtively bypassed giving me an answer altogether.

"I don't mean this to sound like a line or anything, but you have a really beautiful smile, Toni," he remarked like he had been holding in telling me that for a while.

"That's years of braces and thousands on dental work. My teeth were throwing up gang signs like the one you just painted over at the school when I was younger," I said honestly which he found very funny.

"They weren't that bad. Didn't even take away from how pretty you were back then. I mean, still are because again…wow," he said almost blushing. And even though I could tell he was being genuine, it was sometimes still hard to accept that I was considered attractive now because I was a *very* late bloomer. And despite what he'd just said my teeth were tragic until I got health insurance of my own because my mother couldn't afford all the corrective surgeries I needed as a single parent.

And right when I was about to thank him once again, the hairs on the back of my neck suddenly stood proudly as I realized what he'd actually just said. The only social media that I used was LinkedIn and there were certainly no *before* pictures of me on there to show any newcomers my old smile.

"How do you know what my teeth used to look like?" I asked feeling like I hadn't done quite enough homework on him after all and those serial killer thoughts were resurfacing.

"Okay I have a little confession to make," he said still coming off as sane so I allowed him to further explain himself before running for the hills. "We may have only just officially met last week, but I've had the biggest crush on you since I was about fourteen."

"Arlan, what are you talking about? When you were fourteen, I was twenty-one and away in college."

"Yeah I remember you were an hour away at Pomona," he said which almost freaked me out until he continued, "but every now and then you would find your way back to Lakewood to have lunch in the cafeteria with your mom who wasn't just my friend Dave's guidance counselor. She was mine too and I was there. And I saw you," he said with so much emotion that I knew he wasn't making it up. He had really seen me before and it'd apparently left a lasting impression on him.

"And don't worry, I haven't been stalking you since then or anything like that, but when Jill asked if I could do the mural and I saw that you were working here like your mother did, I knew I wanted to see you again. You were the girl in the picture on Ms. Riley's wall in the same spot as your quote now. I remember looking at it and wanting to know you and wishing I was older every time I went to her office. But I was just a kid then so I knew it wasn't possible. But I'm all grown up now and you're…" he paused as he let his eyes envelop me again. "You're still the same as I remember. *Better*," he said breathily and to take my mind off of that tingly feeling he was causing between my thighs I said the first thing that came to mind.

"So you knew my mother?"

"Knew her is putting it

lightly. I owe everything I have to Ms. Riley because my whole life is a fluke. I was an average baseball player, but I was still crushed when the scouts showed no interest in me. I wanted to give up applying to college altogether, but she wouldn't stand for me just bumming it out and becoming a statistic. She remembered my old paintings from art class and pushed me to apply to art school with them and the rest is history," he said then put his hands in his pockets like he didn't know what to do with them.

Or like he was trying his best to keep them under control lest they get a mind of their own and reach out to touch me.

Out of nowhere I was feeling…everything. I was immensely flattered that somebody had looked at me back then and seen something special when even I couldn't. And then I was uneasy because all afternoon I had been imagining myself having back-bending orgasms with a man that I knew I would never again see in this lifetime. I had just wanted the moment, not the man. But it seemed like he wanted me to have both.

My brain was saying all the words, but they still wouldn't come out and since it seemed like he hated silence as much as I did he began speaking again.

"I have one more thing to confess to you, Toni. I left out something when I explained why I was still single. The truth is that it's because I've been comparing all of my relationships to that feeling you gave me as a kid and I know it's crazy to compare them to somebody that I had never even spoken to until last week, but it's what happened. I could never stop myself from thinking about how different things would be if I had you in my life."

For some reason coming to grips with me being somebody's dream girl or *the one who got away* was difficult to grasp, but thinking that he would soon find out I wasn't nearly worth all the hype he'd built up in his mind was incredibly easy to accept. And before he found that out and regretted all those years of pining away for me, I wanted to get out of here before I blew it.

"Arlan, this is a lot to take in so I think we should probably call it a night here," I told him as I struggled to untie the knot on the apron. He accepted my decision with a nod then came to undo it for me.

"C'mon, I'll walk you out," he said softly as he looked down at his feet instead of me.

After my shawl was securely

wrapped around me again by his front door, I used both hands to bring his handsome face down to me so that I could plant a kiss on his cheek.

"You are such a sweet man, Arlan, but we're in two different places in life and I can't pretend like the age thing wouldn't eventually bother me."

"But why? I'm old enough to drink, drive, vote, and rent a car so I should be old enough to be your man too, Toni," he said standing his ground and refusing to let me off so easily.

"And just how do you know I even want a man right now?" I countered thinking that he would give up, but he didn't.

"Well maybe you don't. But I'm ready to concede that you were right when you said that some beautiful moments could be planned. And you could use somebody like me around, somebody who's willing to plan moments like tonight for you to collect when you need one," he said as he leaned down and planted a soft kiss on my temple.

"Just promise you'll at least think about it because I have spray paint up there too and I'm not above personally messing up the mural so I'll have an excuse to see you again, Toni," he said half-seriously which made me smile.

"Please don't. It's really nice and Jill loves it."

"Then promise me."

"I'll think about it," I told him honestly before he opened the door for me. I felt his eyes on my body the whole walk back to my car, but I didn't look back because a big part of me wasn't satisfied with how I was leaving things and still wanted what I had come here for. And that's when I remembered that I had forgotten something inside.

"Hey you forgot your paint," Arlan said holding up the bag I'd left. He signaled that he would bring it out since I was already near my car, but about halfway over to me his curiosity got the best of him and he looked inside. He instantly stopped where he was and looked up at me before finally eliminating those last few feet of space between us.

He was right in front of me, but I was so mortified at what he'd seen that now *I* could only focus on my feet. This humiliation was exactly what I'd deserved for trying to be young, wild, and free on my birthday when I knew I should have been home getting ready for work in the morning.

"I don't know if I should be excited or terrified," he said sounding amused as he put the handle in my hand. "What exactly did you have planned for me tonight because this comes off as more of a *freaky* moment to collect, not a beautiful one," he remarked about the bag full of baby wipes, condoms, and edible paint.

"Well I told you my paint was different from yours, didn't I?" I asked while still avoiding eye contact with him.

"Yeah I guess you weren't wrong about that because I didn't even know edible paint was a thing," he said then asked what I already knew was coming next. "You wanted me to eat this off your body?"

"No! I wanted a non-toxic body paint and this was all they had. I was just going to paint you naked and then have sex with you. That's all," I said because that was my kink limit for the night.

"Somebody has seen *Titanic* too many times," he joked and for some reason that made the shyness that I was feeling dissipate. I wanted to show him that this was no laughing matter and that I could and would give him something even more passionate than that selfish Rose could any day.

"No, not on an easel. I wanted to paint *you*, Arlan. Your body," I said as I let my hand go from his face down to his zipper making him inhale sharply. Just like that his smile dropped and was replaced with him sucking his bottom lip into his mouth. "When you invited me here, you knew there was a possibility that we'd have sex, right?"

"I mean I thought about it and I hoped so, but I wouldn't have been disappointed if it didn't happen."

"Well I just had another change of heart and I definitely want it to happen now so can I paint you or not?"

"I don't know. What's in this stuff anyway? Sugar, food

coloring…" he began reading off the list of ingredients, but I feverishly kissed him before he got to the fillers. I took control and boldly turned him around and pressed him up against my car. I knew I had him when he reached behind to sit the paint on the hood of my car so that his hands could be free to rub my back.

"You can go lower," I informed him because it had been too long since I'd been felt up by big strong hands like his. I could tell he was holding back because we were outdoors though.

"Come back inside and I will," he said against my lips as he smiled through the kiss.

"But can I paint you?" I repeated because those were my terms and conditions to resuming our night. I wanted everything I'd planned or nothing.

"Toni, you can do whatever you want with me. Just come back in," he said nodding over to his house. I quickly agreed before he changed his mind even though it didn't seem likely with all the new pep in his step after he put everything back inside the bag.

I'd figured that we would be going back up to the studio, but instead he walked us down a long hall to the first floor master bedroom. It was nearly all white and pristine inside and I remembered just how neatly he kept his art space so I knew that his room must've been his sanctuary.

"We can't do this here. We'll mess everything up."

"I don't care. I've always thought this room could use some color anyway," he said as he closed the door behind me then turned off the main light leaving only a dimmer light source over by his bed.

"I may not be a professional, but even I know that an artist needs good light to work," I told him as I turned it back on.

"I thought I was the teacher

here."

"You are, but I'm the guidance counselor. So now I'm going to guide your hands to exactly where I want them to be," I said as I placed them on my behind. I was moving much more confidently than I felt, but evidently I was pretending very well because he was none the wiser. I was apparently pretending so well that when he asked if he could paint me first I agreed.

"You know that you have to actually get naked for this, right?" he asked when I just stood there and let him grope me.

"I know. It's just that I'm not

exactly a blank canvas."

"Blank canvases are overrated," he said as he used his hands to lift my dress over my hips and eventually over my head. When he had me completely undressed, I felt shy again standing there literally in my birthday suit while he was still fully clothed so I asked him to at least take off his shirt, but he did me one better and began completely stripping down too.

And while I was mentally picking at every perceived flaw of mine, his eyes were excitedly dancing in every direction taking in all of me. And the way he licked his lips when they fell to my lower half almost made me have to cross my legs. He saw it too then took a step closer before frustratingly closing his eyes and standing in place.

"I forgot that I have to paint you first. I really didn't think this all the way through before agreeing to it," he said and we shared a laugh before he spoke to himself. "Be patient. She'll be all yours soon."

Usually I would've thought he was crazy, but knowing that he wanted me so badly actually made my temperature rise higher. And when he finally stepped out of his pants and underwear, I didn't even bother forcing my eyes to stay on his because we both knew that I wanted to see it. And trust me there was a lot to see. It was so long and girthy that I was afraid it could hit the wrong button and reset my entire body.

"Oh no. I don't think the condoms I brought will fit you," I said genuinely worried, but he just chuckled.

"Don't worry. I have that taken care of," he assured me before I decided to grab ahold of it.

It could barely fit in my hand, but I couldn't wait much longer to see if it would also fit in my mouth. It did, but my lips were stretched to the limit so all I could really do was suck on the head and even that was a struggle.

"It's okay. Just take your time and do what you can," he said calmly sounding like a real instructor as he gently moved my bushy hair to the side so that he could watch me. I started to do a much better job after working up enough saliva, but he was still too thick to go much further. He didn't seem to mind though because he looked down at me with lusty fire in his eyes before suddenly pulling my head up.

"Okay that's enough. Anymore of that will have this

night ending too soon," he moaned out before telling me to go lay down on his bed while he opened up the paint.

I watched him dip his middle finger into the blue paint to see how it tasted before he brought everything over to me. I had planned to essentially do paint by numbers with his body when it was my turn, but he really did take the whole thing very seriously. From the beginning he was impatient with the brush so he used his fingers instead and he wouldn't even let me play with him while he painted me with all the colors of the wind.

When he was finished my

breasts were a royal shade of purple and the most beautiful mixes of blue, green and yellow covered my torso and limbs. I let him put it everywhere except for my nether regions because it didn't take a psychic to see Monistat in my future if he got it into the wrong place.

After painting me just the way he wanted, he got up to wipe his hands and even though he was at least a couple feet away, I could still feel his warm fingers on me. The way he looked at me was like he was planting images of what he wanted to do to me now that he was finished, what he had been restraining himself from doing all night or technically for over half of his life.

I knew I wouldn't be getting to paint him just yet because that frenzied look in his eyes told me that it was time.

Despite that he managed to still gently kiss and lick from my neck down to the inviting space between my breasts then down to my stomach, leaving a magnificent swirl of color that was so pretty it didn't even have a name yet. I was sure he would stop there, but his lips continued their trek until they reached my most sensitive spot.

"Yep. This is by far the most

beautiful canvas I've ever worked with," he moaned out, his words dripping with his adulation for me as he finally used his fingers to explore my inner depths.

"Really?" I asked in between groans because I had only noticed that my pesky stretch marks allowed for a slight variation in the color and perceived texture. He was excited about that though and claimed that my body was an abstract masterpiece just like the rest of his art. And for the first time I saw the remarkable beauty that he saw when I looked down at myself. It was true. I was beautiful in every single way.

When he finally put his

mouth to my body, I was sure that I wouldn't make it out of this house alive. But it wasn't until my cup had runneth over and the overflow became too much to handle when I knew that I would be okay with the possibility of death. I was now certain that there could be no better way to go than with my legs wrapped around this man's head as he voraciously feasted on me.

My resurrection came when I felt him teasingly running his condom covered, thick mushroom head up and down my slit before positioning himself to enter me. I had mistakenly thought that I'd already encountered the biggest and baddest of penises in my early twenties, but Arlan proved that assumption wrong with his first few thrusts. It was like he had instantly unlocked the key to another part of me that even *I* wasn't privy to until now.

He seemed to be so entranced at the sight of watching our bodies connect then equally at looking in my eyes to gauge what felt the best to me. If I was being honest it all felt great because he knew exactly how to wield this paintbrush as well and he made sure to only go as deep as I was comfortable with.

I felt like I should have been

doing so much more than holding onto his slick with sweat back, but I was filled to capacity and unable to move much. I just enjoyed myself and took it as best I could as I thought about what new colors we were creating between us.

"Oh my God. Arlan, just like that! Please don't stop! Please! Just like that!" I pleaded out to him with all of my heart and he actually listened and didn't change a thing. He kept the same pace, the same stroke, and the same intensity as he brought me to my peak. And all at once every nerve in my body exploded into the most eruptive orgasm of my life.

I was so spent that I barely heard him ask for permission before he finally let go too.

"Yes!" I shouted because it would be cruel and unusual punishment to further deny him the ecstasy that I was experiencing.

And just like I'd suspected there had been lots of transference of paint from me to him and we had even managed to somehow knock over a couple containers on the floor from how hard we had shaken the bed, but he really didn't seem to care all that much that his room now looked like a troll had thrown up in it.

He just shivered and held onto and kissed me long after he had finished. We were both content with him just resting inside of me as we came back down from cloud nine, but for some reason I was racking my brain trying to remember the last time that I had felt anything even remotely close to this. I gave up pretty soon because I knew something as memorable as this wouldn't take too long to ring a bell.

This was definitely a first.

"So was it a beautiful enough moment for you to collect too?" I asked him when my breathing had nearly returned to its normal rate.

"Yeah and it was the first of thousands more that I *plan* to collect with you."

"Thousands?" I asked in disbelief.

"Hundreds of thousands, Toni," he said doubling down on his intentions for me as he finally exited my body then laid down next to me. "What, you don't believe that I'm serious about you just because we slept together?"

"I don't know," I said honestly because even as amazing as this experience had just been with him, I wasn't the one who'd been building it up in my head for well over a decade like he had. He sighed before getting up and out of bed.

"I was going to save this for when you left, but I need to show you something now."

"What is it?" I asked sitting up as well.

"Just relax and lay back down. Head on the pillow now," he said in a sexy, authoritative tone that I willingly obeyed.

He made a pit stop in the bathroom before I heard his heavy footsteps from above in his studio. A minute later he was holding a midsized easel up in front of his tall, naked body.

"Remember how I told you

that it was frowned upon to hang up your own painting?" he asked and I nodded because it hadn't been that long ago. "Well meet the exception to the rule. *You're* the exception to the rule, Toni, because no matter where I've lived I've always found a special place in my home for this. I just took it down tonight because I knew you would recognize it," he said as he slowly turned it around to reveal an abstract picture of me. The one from my mother's office wall that he had mentioned being infatuated with.

It was breathtakingly beautiful and I couldn't help but notice that it had the same rich colors that we were both currently covered in. He had recreated its essence on my body and I suddenly felt like I could come again at how thoughtful and romantic he was with me.

"This is my first painting, the one that got me into art school. Interested buyers and galleries have been trying to get me to sell it for years now, but a long time ago I promised myself that one day I would be able to give it to you. Until you tonight Toni, this was the most priceless thing I'd ever held and now I want it to be yours. That's how you should know that I meant everything I told you," he said before letting me know that he understood it would take time for my feelings to grow and catch up to his and how he couldn't wait to see them sprout how his had so long ago.

I accepted the thoughtful and cherished gift from him then mused to myself how just this afternoon I'd thought I would never own an Arlan Parks original when now I was the owner of *the very first* Arlan Parks original. I immediately thought of the perfect place to hang it at home since I knew that it would only be temporarily hanging in my office.

I would be packing up everything soon because I had finally just decided that this would be my last school year planning anybody's future other than my own. I would make new plans that I would actually follow through with and some of them might even include the little cutie that had sparked this new feeling in me.

We were both exhausted from our romp so not long after we fell asleep holding onto one another. Several hours passed before I woke up again tangled in him and his sheets.

That was when I noticed that our skin was so close in shade that it was hard to tell where he ended and I began until I fully opened my eyes and noticed that mine was slightly darker. He wasted no time rubbing his morning erection on my thigh then licking some of the dried paint from my collar bone.

"Arlan, we can't. I'm gonna be late for work," I groaned out when I felt his thumb press into my clit and two of his long fingers slide deep inside of me.

"You know how long I've been waiting for this to happen. I don't want it to be over yet," he said sweetly as he kissed the back of my neck then proceeded to bring me to another mind-blowing finish. "Hey when's the last time you called in sick?"

"Never. I don't get sick

during the school year. I get maybe one or two summer colds a year."

"Call in then," he urged as he handed me his phone. "It's too soon for me to ask you to spend your life with me so for now I'm just asking you to spend the day with me, Toni," he said with a look in his eyes that told me he meant it and would make it worth my while again if I did what he wanted.

I could tell that Jill didn't buy my excuse because like I said, I never got sick, so I rushed her off the phone before she could ask me what'd happened on my date with Arlan.

After that we rolled around some more until we were both starving so he ordered in for breakfast. I knew my hair must have looked crazy because I'd gone to bed without securing it and I could feel lots of paint in the back, but he thoughtfully helped me get it out in the shower.

"What are you thinking about?" he asked with a grin when we were done drying off and changing the now Skittles colored sheets on his bed.

"About how we're gonna top this next time."

"We won't be able to. It's just one of those things that falls in your lap," he teased me going back to his original stance.

"What are you thinking about?" I asked flipping the question on him.

"I'm thinking about how you were my muse before I was ever in the same room with you so I'm trying to imagine what I'm about to create now that I've finally been inside of you," he said casually, but it still gave me goosebumps. That and strangely enough the fact that he knew how to fold a fitted sheet just did something for me and I knew that I would be holding onto him just as tightly as he'd been holding onto me for all these years.

And of course a couple

rounds of good sex didn't magically give me all of the answers to my problems because I *still* didn't know what I wanted to do with the rest of my life. But I had a feeling that I wouldn't have to figure it out by myself anymore. Plus now it was my turn to be the meddling friend and start setting up Jill. I would probably start with Arlan's friend Dave since she always did love a man that could cook and there was nothing she'd love more than double dating with me.

But Arlan made me forget all thoughts of Jill when he brought an easel down from the studio and set it up in his room. All I had done was lazily wrap myself up in his new, crisp white sheets, but he said that he wanted to always remember me like this, in a way that a picture couldn't quite capture.

When he was almost finished he showed me beautiful deep shades of brown wrapped in white that represented me and my wild hair. The way he looked at it told me that this would become his new exception to the rule that would replace his old painting of me.

And making up the bed and cleaning his room proved to be a complete waste of our time because all throughout the day I was in the mood to collect more beautiful moments in it with him. Then out of nowhere I remembered that I still hadn't gotten a chance to paint him yet and we had used or spilled everything that I'd brought over.

It was okay though because I knew exactly where to get more so I would definitely be pulling a repeat of the evening in a few weeks for his birthday. And he would love it.

'90S KINDA LOVE *LAY YOUR HEAD ON MY PILLOW*

FOLLOW ME

Thanks for reading! If you don't want to miss out on any updates about future works of mine then find me on all social media platforms as TanSaidWhat.

Visit www.tanzaniaglover.com

And if the cover art took your breath away as much as it did mine, check out the talented artist Scheba Derogene! Thank you so much for bringing this beautiful couple to life!

THANK YOUS

I said that I was done writing dissertations to my family and friends in this section so I'll try to keep this brief especially since my love for them has remained the same since the first time I did this. But I do want to say that I feel like the luckiest person in the world to be able to go on this journey with people who genuinely love and care for me. Because of the immense amount of love and support that I receive from them, I get to do the thing I love most in the world and I'm forever grateful for it.